Dedication

Dedicated to my lovely wife, Margaret. She was
my inspiration for telling this story that all kids
have the potential to go from being labeled a nerd
to a registered nurse, doctor, or even lawyer.

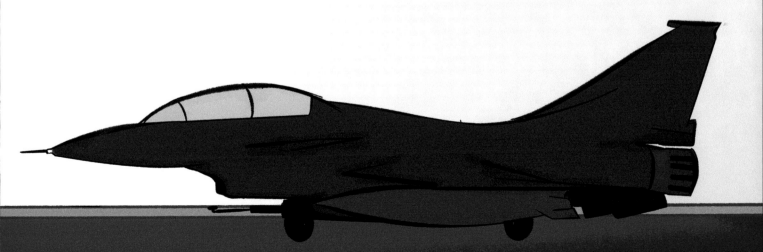

To order additional copies of this book, contact:
Xlibris
844-714-8691
www.Xlibris.com
Orders@Xlibris.com

Text by Wayne Rankin
Illustrations by Dina Soul Writing
Proofreading and Editing by Dina Soul Writing

Library of Congress Control Number: 2022919883
ISBN: Softcover   978-1-6698-5314-5
         Hardcover   978-1-6698-5316-9
         EBook   978-1-6698-5315-2

Print information available on the last page

Rev. date: 10/28/2022

Wayne, the Nerd from Arizona
I'm Wayne
I'm WAYNE
I'm WAYNE
I'M WAYN
I'm WAYNE

"Please, Dad. I want to stay here. I don't want us to move anymore," Wayne begged his dad.

"I'm sorry, buddy. I've been assigned to Spangdahlem Air Base, Germany, and it's an order from my superiors."

Wayne did not want to leave Luke AFB in Phoenix, Arizona. He was born and raised there, and despite the many moves, it was the only place he could call home. He was sad and anxious. Moving so far away would be a great inconvenience.

4

"Couldn't it at least be somewhere closer?" Wayne asked.
"I don't even speak German."

"Our country needs me there, son," his dad replied, ending the
conversation. "They speak English, don't worry," he added.

Wayne knew of his dad's patriotism and discipline.

Within days, Wayne and his dad left Luke AFB in Phoenix, Arizona, not knowing if they would ever return. On a cold afternoon, they landed at Spangdahlem Air Base, Germany.

Spangdahlem Air Base

"We're in this together, buddy," his
dad told him to cheer him up.

"I know, Dad. I know," Wayne replied.

Wayne's first day of school was a disaster. All he could think about was how little he had in common with the other kids.

Why do they look me up and down? Wayne thought every time he felt the gaze of his classmates.

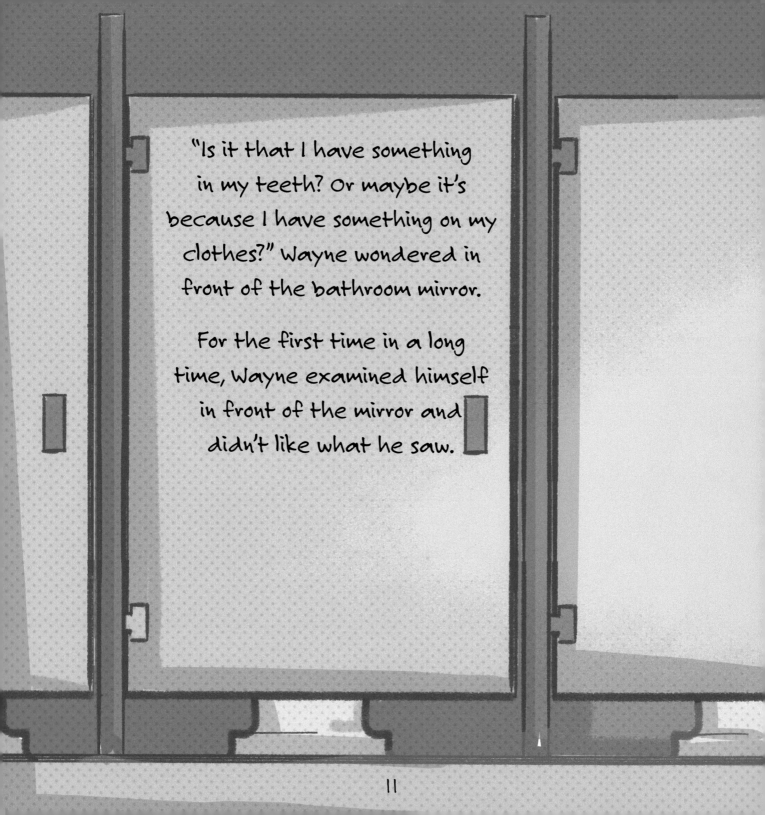

"Is it that I have something in my teeth? Or maybe it's because I have something on my clothes?" Wayne wondered in front of the bathroom mirror.

For the first time in a long time, Wayne examined himself in front of the mirror and didn't like what he saw.

He had pimples on his forehead, crooked teeth, and damaged glasses mended with tape.

"I'm a mess," Wayne said to himself. "No wonder no one wants to get close to me."

13

15

Wayne bit his lip hard; he had never been so frustrated in his life. But at least he had an idea that gave him some strength.

"I've moved three times in the last two years. I just have to wait a bit until we move again."

Wayne thought about turning invisible and expecting the worst, but after a week of sitting alone in the cafeteria, a strange girl with a tomboy look approached him.

"Hi, I'm Anita. I saw you sitting here all alone like a fool and thought I'd come to say hello," she said. From her tone, Wayne couldn't tell if she was being kind or teasing him.

21

"I'm Wayne, the new kid," he said.

"I don't fit in either in this place full of idiots who only care about their parents' rank," Anita said. "And what do I care if your dad is an air force non-commissioned officer or commissioned officer?" So what.

Wayne didn't know what to answer, but he knew very well what Anita was talking about. That was one of the disadvantages of having military parents.

"I like you, Wayne. You don't say much, but you understand everything," Anita said with a smile.

After that, Wayne and Anita sat together in the cafeteria and became good friends.

"DC or Marvel? Pick fast," Anita asked.

"I don't like superhero movies," Wayne admitted. "I prefer Star Wars."

The conversation between them became so heated that a couple of guys sitting near them decided to join in. Soon, the group was growing larger and larger. All attracted to the same nerd's stuff.

After a week, there were already six students sitting at the same table. By the end of the month, there were almost fifteen, and they had to join several tables so that everyone could sit together.

"I've never had so many friends
before," Wayne confessed to
Anita one day at the gym.

"Why?" Anita asked. "You're kind of
dumb, but you're a good kid."

33

Wayne thought about it for quite a while. He knew the answer but was afraid to come clean with Anita.

"People avoid me because of how I dress and because I don't care about the same things they do," Anita confessed.

Wayne was glad she took the first step. "And I have pimples on my forehead, crooked teeth, and my glasses have tape on them," Wayne said with a smile. "So, what does it matter?"

"It doesn't matter at all!" Anita replied.

Wayne, Anita, and the other kids soon became known as the Nerd Squad. It was a nickname the bullies and popular kids gave them to try to make fun of them, but it backfired.

Wayne and Anita loved the name and were now bragging about it.

For the first time in his life, Wayne felt accepted and proud of who he was. Those five years were the happiest of his life, but they came to an end the day his dad told him they were moving again.

Wayne said goodbye to his friends, cried, hugged them, and vowed to keep in touch with them.

"We'll always be a member of the Nerd Squad," Anita encouraged him, "No matter where you are, buddy."

42

Years passed, and although they did not live in the same place, the original Nerd Squad stayed in touch. They all sent each other pictures of their transformations and growth. They were still very good friends.

They all grew up and realized that when we are kids, they call us nerds, but when we are adults, they call us smart.

46

We left behind pimples, crooked teeth, and glasses with tape, and we became lawyers, doctors, nurses, chief executive officers, and even presidents.

Growing up is about changes.
The problems you face growing
up today is temporary.

Just like the caterpillar, you,
too, will change on the inside
and outside for the better.

Stay strong and be true to
yourself and your heart!

Today's nerds have become
tomorrow's leaders.

Wayne is a good kid but has always had a hard time making friends. His dad is an air force master sergeant. He travels a lot, even overseas. Now, Wayne is in a new school and feels unsure of himself. He has pimples on his forehead, crooked teeth, and mended glasses.

Wayne, the nerd, has to deal with his appearance and the challenge of being a wanderer. However, he is not alone; there are others just like him!

Join Wayne on his adventure from Luke AFB Phoenix, Arizona, to Spangdahlem Air Base, Germany, and see his transformation from an ugly caterpillar to an amazing and beautiful butterfly!

Printed in the United States
by Baker & Taylor Publisher Services